D0912982

BLAIR

905 W. Main Street, Suite 19 D-1
Durham, NC 27701

 *Blair is an imprint of Carolina Wren Press.
The mission of Blair/Carolina Wren Press is to
seek out, nurture, and promote literary work
by new and underrepresented writers.*

 *We gratefully acknowledge the ongoing
support of general operations by the Durham
Arts Council's United Arts Fund.*

Library of Congress Control Number: 2020940535
ISBN 13: 978-1-949467-4-13

It wasn't my fault.

It was his.

And his.

And hers!

One day, Dad opened the door and out went Wilhelmina, running after a squirrel.

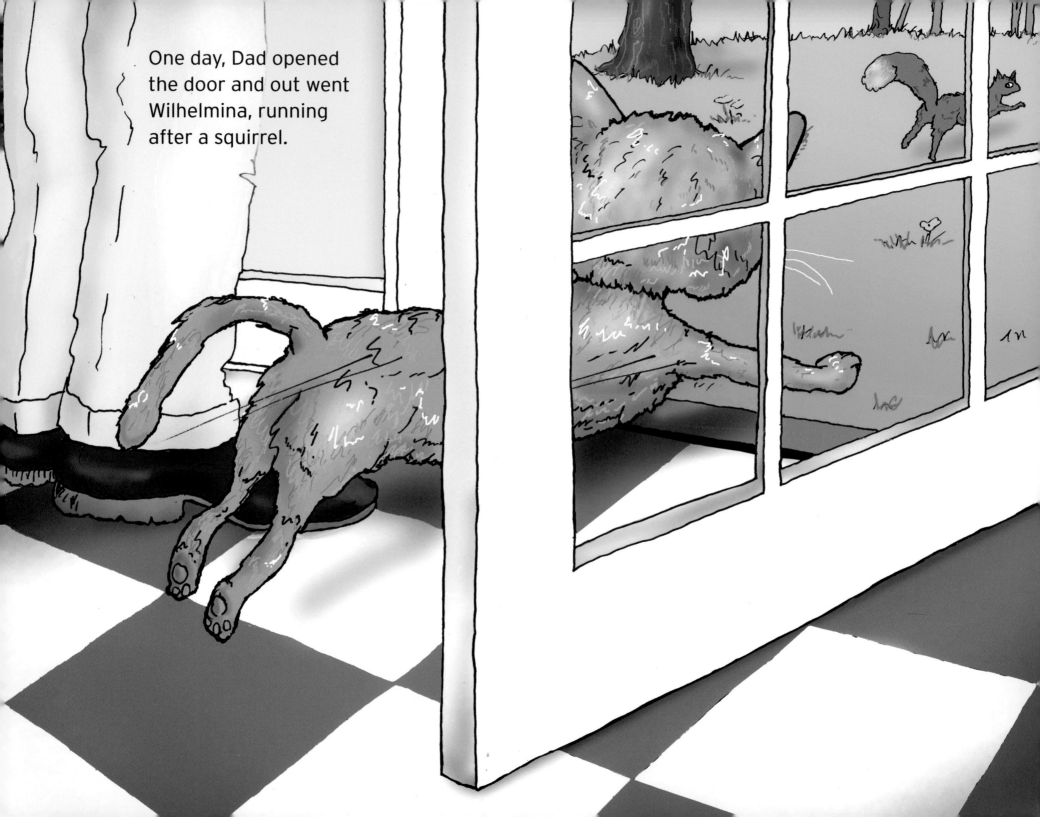

And out we all went, Dad, Papa and me, chasing after Wilhelmina. But cats have four legs and run twice as fast.

Where did she go?

Now my tummy was tumbling, and I started to sweat.
We looked and we looked but without any luck.

Take a nap? Take a nap? Sleep while Wilhelmina's gone?
But . . . What if? What if? What if?

The What-ifs kept coming. They just wouldn't stop.

Then out of nowhere I felt whiskers and a scratchy lick on my cheek.

WILHELMINA!

She came back in the window, just like dad said. After more kisses and hugs, she settled down for a nap. I tiptoed to the kitchen to fix her a snack.

I was happy and humming and feeling so good.
Then I remembered—THE WINDOW!

I DIDN'T CLOSE IT!

So, out we went again—Dad, Papa, and me—looking
for Wilhelmina, wondering where she could be.

Joseph Belisle draws, paints, teaches art, is husband to David and father to Faith, and proudly runs Lighthouse, the LGBTQ+ teen group at Kids In Crisis. He grew up in a big family in a small New England town and currently lives in Fairfield County, CT, where it is his job to keep up with the real-life Wilhelmina.

Acknowledgments

This book was made possible in large part by the love and support of my husband, David. Special thanks to my daughter, Faith, whose real-life experience with her lost cat informed this story. Big shout-outs also go to the people I relied on for advice as this book progressed: all the wonderful folks at Blair, Carol Belisle, Claire Goddu, Cheryl Langevin Alderman, Meira Rosenberg, Marianne McShane, Drew Lamm, Fischer and Ridley Gould, and my young art students who patiently listened to my multiple revisions. This book is dedicated to the memory of my brother, Bob, who taught everyone he met about the importance of fun.

For more information about the famous art included and hinted at in this book, go to www.blairpub.com/wilhelmina-art.